Puffin Books

A GHOST OF A CHANCE

Anne-Marie loves her dog Maudie. To leave her
behind in Australia when she goes to England for a
year is about as much as she can bear. But Anne-
Marie soon becomes caught up in the story of
another girl, many centuries ago, who also misses her
beloved dog – a mysterious white ghost dog who
beckons to Anne-Marie, asking her for help . . .

Also by Nette Hilton

Picture books
The Long Red Scarf
A Proper Little Lady
Would You?
Tough Lester

For young readers
Four Eyes
Hiccups
Friday Card
The Web
The Belonging of Emmaline Harris
The New Kid
Strays
Napoleon

For older readers
Hothouse Flowers
Square Pegs
Clouded Edges

A Ghost of a Chance

Nette Hilton

Illustrated by
Chantal Stewart

Puffin Books

Puffin Books
Penguin Books Australia Ltd
487 Maroondah Highway, PO Box 257
Ringwood, Victoria 3134, Australia
Penguin Books Ltd
Harmondsworth, Middlesex, England
Penguin Putnam Inc.
375 Hudson Street, New York, New York 10014, USA
Penguin Books Canada Limited
10 Alcorn Avenue, Toronto, Ontario, Canada M4V 3B2
Penguin Books (N.Z.) Ltd
Cnr Rosedale and Airborne Roads, Albany, New Zealand
Penguin Books (South Africa) (Pty) Ltd
4 Palinghurst Road, Parktown 2193, South Africa

First published by Penguin Books Australia, 1998

3 5 7 9 10 8 6 4 2

Copyright © Nette Hilton, 1998
Illustrations Copyright © Chantal Stewart, 1998

Designed by Scott Williams, Penguin Design Studio
Typeset in 12/16pt Sabon by Post Pre-press Group, Brisbane
and Midland Typesetters, Maryborough, Victoria
Made and printed in Australia by Australian Print Group

National Library of Australia
Cataloguing-in-Publication data:

Hilton, Nette, 1946– .
A ghost of a chance.

ISBN 0 14 038 795 1.

I. Stewart, Chantal. II. Title.

A823.3

For all my English friends, Father Trevor, Gillian and Elliott, Sybil and all the staff and students of St Andrews School, North Weald. Thank you for making 1994 so truly unforgettable.

And to Carolyn and Nicola, whose house I have once again borrowed for Anne-Marie and her Aussie mum and dad. Special thanks for being brave enough to take on an Aussie farm in the middle of cane fields.

And always – to my family who let me wander off and live my dreams.

My gentle Puck, come hither.

A Midsummer Night's Dream (2.I.148)

Before . . .

She's very happy and looks wonderful with the little red bows in her hair, Nan had written. Anne-Marie wasn't sure about the little red bows. Maudie never seemed to like them very much when they'd both been at home together. *And she snuggles down every night without a fuss.*

She's missing you . . . Pop had added in his funny, squiggly writing at the bottom of the letter . . . *but I tell her every day that it won't be long before you come home.*

Anne-Marie held the letter in her hands. The writing went all misty and made blotches on some of the words when a tear slid down her nose and landed – splat! – on the paper.

It *would* be long.

It would be *for ever*.

And Maudie was such an old, old dog. Anne-Marie was already ten years old and Maudie arrived on her first birthday. That was old for a dog.

'You can't take her all the way to England with us,' her dad had explained. 'She's getting on a bit and it wouldn't be fair to lock her into the back of a plane for so long. And . . .' he continued when Anne-Marie said that she would be all right if they packed some of her toys, or the old jumper with the horse on the front that used to be Anne-Marie's when she was little. (Maudie loved that jumper. It was with her now in the bottom of the basket in Nan's kitchen.) 'And . . . there's quarantine. Dogs can't go from one country to another without staying in a special place to make sure they're well.'

'Of course she'd be well!' Anne-Marie couldn't understand why she would be sick. Maybe a little bit sick from the plane. *She'd* got sick on that, but locked up in quarantine?

'It's the law,' her mum said. 'It happens to all animals from overseas. Think about it, Anne-Marie,' her mother had gone on. 'Maudie is getting to be an old dog now.'

Maudie *was* getting to be an old dog. Anne-Marie didn't think she could bear it if Maudie died and she was all the way over the sea in this strange, cold country. Maudie'd think that Anne-Marie didn't care. She would think she'd forgotten all about her.

She lay down on the bed with her head in the spot where Maudie would have been and waited for the year to go by.

She could stand it if Maudie was here.

A year was *for ever*.

Already they'd been in England halfway to for ever and it was only February. It had been December when her mum had left their school in Australia to start work in a school here, and it was a whole long time till next December when she'd stop work and they'd go on the plane again over oceans and continents, taking them back home to Australia.

Anne-Marie's heart sagged a little in her chest. So long before she would feel days that were hot and long and white, and hear the cicadas in the trees and touch the cool froth of waves that foamed over her feet.

So long before she'd see Nan and Pop again.

And Maudie.

She'd found a fluff of Maudie's grey hair tangled in the sleeve of a jumper, a little tuft that might have come from the fuzzy part on her back. It had somehow survived the washing and cleaning and packing. It was still Maude's colour and Anne-Marie had sniffed it. But the smell had gone.

The wonderful old doggy smell that was Maude.

'That dog pongs!' her mother used to say. 'And look at the mess she's made on your bed.' But she wasn't really cross. They'd made a Maudie patch with an old towel to protect the doona, and given her another bath.

And there she'd be again. The next night. And every night, snoozing, snoring, warming the bottom of Anne-Marie's bed.

But nobody warmed the bottom of Anne-Marie's bed now. Maudie instead learned to live in a basket in the kitchen at Nan's house. And she was brushed and bathed and clipped.

Chapter One

Father Tom was waiting for Anne-Marie under a gateway that had a little roof. Behind him the tall, square tower of the church loomed up against the grey sky. The church was all built of tiny red bricks with arched windows along its sides which were coloured in darkly with pieces of glass that made story pictures from the Bible.

And in front of it all, sprinkled across the churchyard like teeth in an old mouth, were gravestones. Lots and lots of gravestones.

The only gravestones that Anne-Marie had ever seen were in a cemetery in Australia and they didn't even have a church next door. They had been white and clean and looked almost as if they were sunbaking under the blue, blue sky. Not like these ones at all. Here they were stuck up any old way, some leaning over, some bowing forward and some with so many dark patches of inky moss growing on them they looked more like a mound of earth than a great, heavy lump of stone. Some of them had their own special angels with their wings spread wide, and all of them, every last one, slept in the secret silence of the village church above them.

'This is the churchyard.' Father Tom stood with his arms folded across the middle part of his lean body. His long black coat had lots of buttons all the way up the front that made him look even taller and thinner than he really was.

He was still taller by far than the other teachers at her school and was easily seen as he strode along the corridor to the classrooms for his own special lessons. He liked to talk and Anne-Marie had discovered that she liked to listen.

He had told her all about his two dogs. 'Perhaps you'd like to come over to the vicarage and meet them?' he'd said. 'And we can go for a walk to the church. There's something there that I think you'll really like. I think . . .' he'd added quietly, '. . . it will make you feel better, too.'

So Anne-Marie's mum had dropped her at the gate where Father Tom was waiting to tell her about his church. Sometimes he said some funny things in the middle of everything else. 'Later, when the weather warms up a bit . . .' he was saying, '. . . we have tug-of-war games over these headstones. Do you do that in Australia?'

Tug-of-war over headstones? Anne-Marie didn't think so. But it certainly sounded like it could be a lot of fun.

'Some of these are hundreds of years old,' Father Tom said and then stopped. 'There's even one headstone with a skull and crossbones on it. Do you want to see it?'

Anne-Marie hurried along to look. This would be something to tell her friends in Australia about in her next letter. A real skull and crossbones!

The vicar was already disappearing around

the corner of the church, and the churchyard suddenly seemed very quiet. The trees crowded together, branches mixed in with each other, and so bare that birds' nests were able to be seen mingled in amongst them.

But there were no birds in there.

And the sky overhead was low and gloomy and the afternoon, still only four o'clock, was already disappearing into evening.

Anne-Marie looked up again at the cold, bricked tower and the tiny dark windows that were cut in its sides.

'A priest used to live up there, a long time ago.'

Anne-Marie nearly jumped out of her skin when the vicar spoke.

'You must be frozen,' he went on. 'Come into the church. It won't be much warmer but I think you're going to like what I have to show you.'

Anne-Marie stayed close.

It wasn't just the stillness, though, or the mist that was twirling its long fingers out from behind the headstones to creep up and under the trees that made her want to hurry a little.

It was another feeling, as if whatever it was she was going to see had been waiting for her.

Chapter Two

Anne-Marie had been in other churches in England. She'd visited them with her mother and father.

She'd breathed the coldness in their air and felt tiny under their great vaulted ceilings of stone, webbed and woven to look like the bellies of whaling boats, or the Club boat the lifesavers used at her beach back home.

She'd walked on the stone floors of these churches and discovered that, beneath them, in an icy place, lay the bones of ancient people. Kings and queens and great lords and ladies sleeping a sleep that had lasted for centuries.

She'd liked none of those churches. Not even Westminster Abbey in London and its magnificent Christmas Nativity with Baby Jesus snug in his manger bed. But this village church, this little tiny church, felt different. It was just as cold and the stone floor was still hard and clattery against her shoes and the light through the windows still shone eerily into the gloom, but it seemed to welcome her and draw her on, closer and further into a little room set off to the side.

Perhaps it was the way Father Tom flicked on a light and tidied a kneeling cushion as he came through that made it feel so friendly.

'It's darker over here,' he said as he walked past the pews and turned to the small area. 'There's still enough light for you to see though.'

Anne-Marie followed. She felt that she could have hurried past him and led the way herself, so sure was she of where they were going.

'Have you seen a chapel before?' Father Tom slowed down.

Anne-Marie stopped.

Ahead of her she could see a smaller room set apart from the rest of the church by a pillar and a small carved fence. It was a special place: a place where ancient families sometimes lay in tombs that sat high on stone ledges. She could see Father Tom dusting the statue that decorated the top of one now.

This was the place where her feet were hurrying to go.

'They're not really statues,' Father Tom was explaining. 'They're called effigies. You see, there were no cameras back then. This was just a way of showing people who was buried here.'

Anne-Marie shivered. She didn't like to think about the great, stone box that waited ahead of her.

But still, her feet itched to go on and she crept further into the shadows of the tiny chapel. She stood perfectly still and looked at the high platform, and the box above it – a bed for the carved figure lying there with her head on a pillow that would never be soft. But still she slept on, with her hands folded over her breast of stone and her long skirt rippling into gentle creases that would be hard and cold to touch.

There was something else too. Something in the shadows, there. Near the end of the great box bed, right where the feet should be.

Anne-Marie stepped forward, not looking at the other two longer boxes that were tucked neatly beneath their own deeply coloured windows.

'Who is she?' she asked.

'Well . . .' Father Tom stood back, 'aren't you a clever one. This is exactly the one I wanted to show you.' He moved to make room for Anne-Marie so she could stand on the step beside him. 'This is Lady Jane Latimer.'

Anne-Marie looked down from the top step, at the sleeping carved stone that was Lady Jane Latimer.

She had a small face, a young face, with hair that hung in thick stone curls around her shoulders. Her eyes were closed, as if in sleep, and

beneath her folded hands she held a cross and a book. There was something else too, something that looked like a tiny latched circlet. Flowers, stone flowers, were sprinkled around her skirts and into her hair.

Anne-Marie looked at her and was filled with a great sadness. She longed to reach out and hold the cold stone hands the way her own mother did when Anne-Marie felt sad. But this time, Anne-Marie knew, the sadness wasn't an inside thing.

This time she was feeling the sadness that belonged to another person who had lived centuries before.

'Oh . . .' Anne-Marie's voice crept out of her mouth. 'Why is she so *sad*?'

Father Tom touched Lady Jane's stone face. 'I don't know,' he said and moved slightly, his hand brushing a cobweb from her skirt. It was then that Anne-Marie saw it.

There, right there at her feet, was another statue. A proper, sitting up statue.

It was a dog, a little dog with long waves in his curly hair and a tongue that lolled out happily as if he was ready, as soon as his mistress woke, to play a game. Anne-Marie could easily imagine him with a ball.

'I thought you'd like it,' Father Tom was saying.

'See . . .' he pointed to the other tombs. 'When important people died, statues of animals were often placed at their feet.'

Anne-Marie looked at the other effigies in the chapel. A deer sat quietly at the feet of the lady, and a great proud dog sat at the feet of the lord.

'They are Lady Jane's parents,' Father Tom went on. 'They were very important people who lived here hundreds of years ago. You can still see the manor house that they lived in. It's on the other side of Ellersham Forest, not far from where you live. Deserted, now. Great big old mansions like that one cost so much money to keep them repaired. Of course it's falling down now but you can still see the way it used to be and the Forest hasn't grown back up over the clearing at the front of the house. Once it would all have been lawns and gardens – a great place for running about.'

Anne-Marie looked again at the little dog, the rousy-tousy dog lying at Lady Jane's feet, who was waiting to play.

'Was Lady Jane important?' she asked.

'I expect so,' Father Tom said. 'Only important people were treated this way.'

'Then why is she so sad?' Anne-Marie climbed up onto the step again, and again she was filled with the sadness of the statue. 'Why *is* she so sad?'

Father Tom went on straightening some of the kneeling cushions, just like he might have done in his own lounge room. 'Well, the plague that killed them all was a terrible thing,' he explained. 'Whole families, just like hers, died of a horrible disease many centuries ago. A dreadful time . . .' He brightened up. 'I thought you might like to see her little dog, though. I didn't intend to make *you* sad.'

Anne-Marie turned around. 'It's a nice little dog,' she said. 'My dog likes to sleep near my feet too.'

She turned again, her eyes seeking the tiny animal statue, but it was the sleeping girl on the bed of stone, with long hair and neatly folded arms that called her back.

'Come along then,' Father Tom was moving towards the heavy wooden door. 'Best we leave her again in peace.'

Anne-Marie didn't want to leave. For some reason she wanted to stay a little longer and was turning slowly to clamber down from the step when she thought she smelt something. A perfume. One that belonged somehow to the earth but was sweet and clinging – one that she knew.

She sniffed, checking back out into the light to see if perhaps Father Tom was spraying some air freshener. But Father Tom was checking one of the hymn books that seemed to be losing its cover.

She breathed again. Sniffing. Out there in that lighted part of the church there was nothing.

She turned back into the darkness, into the deeper gloom of the chapel, with the sky beyond the window too dark now to make any colours in the leadlight window.

And still the perfume called her, filling her with its soft sweetness and touching all around her with its scent.

Her heart, for a reason that she couldn't find, was beating too fast. There was nothing here to hurt her.

Stronger the scent called, and Anne-Marie found herself moving closer again to the steps and the statue of Lady Jane Latimer.

Here the perfume was sweetest. Anne-Marie stood for a moment, feeling the warmth of it. She let her eyes travel the length of Lady Jane's stone skirt to the dog on his fat, padded cushion with the tassel that hung down to one side.

All stone.

All cold.

And all of it perfumed.

She looked more closely at the dog. Perhaps someone had filled a vase with flowers and put it down there near his feet.

But there was nothing except a crack. She'd not noticed before but now that she looked, searching for the reason for the scent, she saw the cruel line that started at the dog's paw.

Soon it would open up.

The dog seemed to laugh at her, and Anne-Marie tried to think of his eyes and the way his mouth tweaked up at the corners.

And not the way the crack would spread and turn the lovely, happy stone animal to dust.

Chapter Three

Anne-Marie wrote to Nan as soon as she got home. She told her about the gravestones and how people played tug-of-war over them in summer. She told her about the church and how it was centuries old, and she told her about Father Tom.

She didn't tell her about Lady Jane Latimer though.

She tried to, but whenever she thought of the little dog at her feet and the awful crack that she'd seen, she felt again the sadness that seemed to belong to Lady Jane. How strange that she used to live in a house that was so close.

How strange this place was, now her home for the rest of the year. So many tiny houses standing tall, side to side like soldiers in a row, with neat winding paths running along in front of them. A tidy little pocket of modern houses in clean red brick with tiled roofs, set between the Forest and a village that looked like it had just stepped out of the pages of a picture book. Shops that were white and snowy with criss-cross patterns of timber on them – Tudor style her mother had said. And they were *old* houses – some still with stables for horses and coaches that hadn't come this way for many, many years, and all of them tucked up snug and tight for winter.

Anne-Marie looked out her bedroom window.

From here she could see across the lawn with its threadbare trees to where the Forest began on the other side of the road. It wasn't like Australian bush. In Australian bush you could get lost; you could walk for hours and hours and not see another house or a car or a road. But Ellersham Forest had a beginning and an end – a haircut of trees parted by a road that ran through it, with occasional bald patches where villages grew and fields lay waiting for spring. It had a path right through the middle of it that led to the next village.

And the manor house where Lady Jane Latimer used to live.

Anne-Marie stood on tiptoe. It was too dark to see the other end of the Forest. She couldn't have seen the manor house anyway. It was further away. But not too far to ride there on her bike.

She couldn't seem to stop thinking about Lady Jane and her tiny dog. What happened to her little dog? Who looked after it for her?

Father Tom hadn't known. Maybe one of the servants looked after it – like Nan was looking after Maudie.

She'd think about it tomorrow.

For now, there was Maudie's new coat and a collar waiting to be wrapped up and put in a parcel.

Anne-Marie touched it, ran her hands over the warm woollen back of the coat and tried to imagine Maude's fat, old wriggly body in there.

She tried hard but somehow it was just a coat and, even with her eyes shut, it didn't feel like a dog.

It was just as lifeless as the statue that lay at Lady Jane's feet. She thought it might help if she stuffed Maudie's coat with tissue paper but then, right when her mother was calling her to hurry up and have her shower, she had a better idea. Quickly she got undressed and stuffed her dirty socks inside the new doggy coat before she dived under the hot shower. It still didn't look like a Maudie shape but at least whenever Maudie dressed up in her coat she'd get a whiff of Anne-Marie.

'Don't be too long,' Anne-Marie's mum peered through the steam in the bathroom. 'It's school tomorrow.'

Anne-Marie didn't answer.

Another whole week of school, another whole week of doing maths like she'd never done before! Another week of being alone. And different.

She turned off the shower and reached out into the warm steam for her towel.

She'd try not to think about it. There was absolutely nothing she could do even if she did think about it.

She couldn't help being Australian and having a voice that sounded different and using the wrong words for things.

'Not chips!' the kids at school would say. 'They're *crisps*!'

And they'd scold her in voices that sounded as strange to her as hers did to them. It would do no good to fight about it – fighting wouldn't change anything.

She'd never grow out of being Australian. And they'd always be English.

Around her the steam cooled and Anne-Marie pulled on her pyjamas.

Nothing was going to make a difference. It would never change.

She just wanted to go back home.

She wanted to see Nan and Pop.

She wanted her dog Maude.

In big letters, with her finger, Anne-Marie wrote a message in the misty mirror. A message to nobody because nobody would be able to read it when the air cleared.

I miss Maude, she wrote.

'Hurry up!' The door whooshed open and billows of steam sucked out into the hall. Anne-Marie's mum stood there. 'Go and snuggle into bed before you get cold.'

Anne-Marie hugged down tight in her bed. Her toes reached right to the end. Her feet bumped against Maudie's dog coat where it lay full of her dirty socks and she thought of Lady Jane, with her feet touching the statue of her little dog.

'Who's Puck?'

Anne-Marie looked up. Her mother was standing in the doorway.

'Who?' she said.

'Puck. You wrote a message in the mirror that says "I miss Puck".'

Anne-Marie felt her heart give a little bumpy beat. 'I didn't write that,' she said. 'I wrote "I miss Maude".'

Her mother collected up some of the clothes that had fallen to the floor. 'Well, it's pretty strange writing. I was sure you had written "Puck".'

'Puck?' Anne-Marie tested it out, and felt another little bump near her heart. 'I don't even know what it means.'

'It's a very old-fashioned name,' her mother said. 'It was the name of somebody in a play . . .'

'Could it be the name of a dog, do you think?' Anne-Marie thought about her visit to the church. She remembered touching the small stone dog with the smiling mouth, and the scent that surrounded her as she'd done so.

Had Lady Jane Latimer whispered the name to her then, in the scent of the flowers? She wondered about that name hiding inside her until she let it go, trickling out the end of her finger onto the misty mirror.

Anne-Marie climbed out of bed. 'I just want to see,' she explained to her mum as she brushed by. 'I was sure I wrote Maude.'

'Perhaps you were thinking about something else,' her mother said. 'It's an unusual name and it has a nice sound. Perhaps you heard it at school today.'

Anne-Marie looked at the fading letters in the mirror.

I miss Puck.

There it was. Just as her mother had said.

'Whatever made you write it, I wonder.' Her mum was watching her in the mirror behind the words.

Anne-Marie smiled. 'I think it was something I heard in the church today.' She climbed back into bed and hugged the blankets close. 'I think it's the name of a dog.'

'I'll bet Father Tom told you that.' Her mother leaned down for a goodnight kiss. 'He loves talking about animals.'

Anne-Marie checked back.

No. No, he definitely hadn't told her.

But somebody had.

'Who'd want to call their dog Puck?' Her dad appeared, his hand ready to switch out the light.

Anne-Marie wondered again about the scent that had whispered silently to her in the chapel. She wondered if she should have been scared. It was such a ghostly thing to happen.

But she wasn't scared. Not one bit.

Instead she felt just a teensy bit excited. And just a teensy bit nervous when she thought about who might call their dog such a strange, old name.

Chapter Four

Back home in Australia there was a house on a hill where nobody lived. It stood empty and eerie, staring out at the setting sun, and Anne-Marie could easily imagine the darker shadows being wonderful homes for slithery things – creatures that moved with the merest rustle and whose bodies shone round and fat even when there was no light to polish them.

She had gone to this house with her mother and had stood outside, not too close in case whatever it was that was watching her from under the sagging veranda just might slime out and tangle around her ankles. She hadn't liked it and was happy when her mother turned to go back home. She remembered hurrying over the long, whispering grass and was panting when the taller eucalypts and clumpier rainforest trees had covered them in shadow.

She had never gone back. And now, as she pedalled her bike along the path through this very different Ellersham Forest in England she was glad bike riding was still something that took a lot of concentration so she didn't have time to think too hard about that other house.

A tree with long, bare fingers reached out to snatch at her hair, and roots set traps to try and tip her, but Anne-Marie didn't slow down. She pedalled hard, ready for the climb up the last little hill before the end of the Forest. It was all so different from riding at home where the tracks beneath her tyres were hard-baked yellow and gravelly. Even in winter in Australia the water lay in neater puddles with edges and bottoms that were pebbled and hard. Not here. Grass as green and thick and wet as moss on a rock soaked itself to the ground waiting for a foot or a tyre to venture across it. Then it sagged and spilled itself over shoes or rubber, leaving mud-caked waves to show where it had been. And above it all were trees with strange names – horse chestnuts, oaks – empty of their leaves and dark-stained with damp. So many trees crowded closely together and still the sky was able to be seen between their branches. Australian trees bunched their leaves tightly onto *their* branches and twigs and kept the sky out – no matter how hard you looked.

Her bike wobbled and then bogged itself in deeper leaf mould, mud and a tree root that had crept out to hog the path, so Anne-Marie reluctantly gave up and climbed off. She stood still for a minute, catching her breath, getting ready to climb the last little hill. Behind her the Forest clambered up the rise like a gang of school kids crowded too closely together – lumping and bumping any which way. All the branches reached out to each other and all the trunks were dressed in velvety green moss.

In front of her, behind a gate with *'Trespassers will be prosecuted'* written on a sign attached to it, stood a large, empty field. The soil was belly-up, waiting, her dad had said, for the farmer to plant in spring. Beyond it was the motorway with model-sized cars zooming silently by. The sound, so incredible back there on the pedestrian overpass that Anne-Marie had hurried to be rid of it, didn't reach out this far.

She turned back to the rise and pushed her bike free. Beyond it, just up there over the ridge, was where Lady Jane's house would be.

'You can see it . . .' her dad had said, '. . . when you get to the top. Just follow the path down and then turn to the right.' He'd offered to come with her but Anne-Marie had said no. This time, she decided, she wanted to go by herself.

Anne-Marie didn't look up when she got to the top of the hill. Instead she looked along the path that wound down ahead of her and veered off to the right as her dad had said. She let her eyes lift up then, up above the branches and,

30

right when she least expected it, she saw the manor house. And it was not a bit, not one bit, like the house in Australia.

There it stood, alone in the middle of a cleared section of the hill. Even the Forest had not dared to grow too close and clustered around the bottom of the rise that belonged to Hollingsworth House.

Anne-Marie rode down, quickly so she could get there faster and make sure her eyes were not playing tricks on her.

It wasn't like *any* house that Anne-Marie had seen before. It was enormous, with broken walls and strange arched peaks like steepled fingers pointing to the sky. Empty climbing plants huddled close against its sides, clambering through holes that had been windows and peeking out through bigger holes that had been doors.

The house had no roof. There was only the sky with its gloomy grey clouds that seemed almost to touch the top of the walls. Yet it stood so proudly on top of its hill, with its feet in the stone rubble that had been part of its walls, and Anne-Marie wondered if it was, in fact, like Sleeping Beauty's castle and was only waiting for its time to start again.

Anne-Marie realised then that the afternoon

was shadowing itself towards evening. She didn't think she'd like to be here when it got dark – then it might not be so easy to think kindly about such an immense, cold giant of a house.

And the Forest behind her wouldn't be as friendly in the dark either, even though a lot of villagers liked to come out at the end of the day, walking dogs all decked out in coats to keep them warm. Maudie would like the Forest. She would have liked this enormous old house too, with walls that hid places for rabbits and squirrels to play.

The ground looked so grassy and green here, where the Forest had stayed back. Maybe the Forest just knew it wasn't supposed to grow in a place that had been a lawn such a long, long time ago.

Lady Jane Latimer would have played here with her little dog.

Anne-Marie kicked hard at the grass. It was soggy, and a great big dollop clung to the front of her shoe. It was dumb! Dumb! Dumb! It was dumber even thinking about games that she could play when *her* dog wasn't here.

Her dog was all the way across the world in Australia!

Her dog would probably forget her before she ever even got back home!

She kicked the grass again but this time she just let the mud hang on. It was too awful to think about Maudie forgetting her. More than anything Anne-Marie just wanted to hold her, to make sure that Maude *wouldn't* forget, and that she'd still be there when the plane finally landed. Waiting, panting and wriggling her fat bottom the way she did when she was excited.

'Hey! What are you doing here?'

Anne-Marie jumped. She got such a fright she nearly dug her foot in up to her ankle.

'Did you lose your way then?' Edward, a boy from school, whooshed past her and did a big wheelie, then let his bike drop to the ground.

'I wanted to see the manor house,' Anne-Marie said. She didn't tell him about the girl who'd lived here all that long time ago. Or the little stone dog. Or the strange name that her mother had read on the mirror.

'Don't get in my way then,' Edward was busy juggling a ball out from under his anorak. It amazed Anne-Marie that he'd actually got it to fit up there. 'I'm going to have a game of football.'

'Who with?'

'Just me.' Edward kicked the ball and it breezed further up the rise and bounced once on the ground before disappearing through a gap in the wall of Hollingsworth House.

Edward stood still. He looked at his feet as if they might help out by walking forward a little, but he didn't move. 'It's the third ball I've lost this year!' he said and he began to turn away. 'I'll really cop it when I get home.'

Anne-Marie looked at the doorspace. It was very dark inside.

'All you have to do is go through there,' she said. 'You can get it from the other side.'

Edward looked at the doorspace but he didn't move any closer to the deep, waiting shadows. He looked very miserable.

'Oh, come on!' she said. 'I'll go in with you.'

The ball had gone right through the gap and rolled to the bottom of some old, stone stairs.

Anne-Marie and Edward looked at the stairway and then at the ball that had rolled all the way down to the bottom.

'I'm not going down there,' Edward said. 'I'll come back tomorrow and get it.'

'It'll be just the same tomorrow. There's nothing to hurt you.'

It *was* dark down there though.

And it was getting darker outside. The clouds had formed themselves into a low, clumpy grey ceiling above them – the sort of clouds that might grumble out thunder at any minute.

'I have to go home,' Anne-Marie heard herself saying and tried not to think about the ride through the Forest with the sky so dark and glooming out thunder. The dogs and their owners would all have gone home if she didn't hurry and she didn't want to ride past all those trees with their long stick fingers and frowning trunk faces by herself.

'What about my ball?' Edward said. 'I don't want to go in by myself and get it.'

Anne-Marie looked again at the path and the place where it disappeared into the twisted branches of the Forest trees. 'I have to go,' she said as she ran to her bike.

Edward didn't say anything. Anne-Marie saw him climb back out onto the path and collect his bike. He wheeled it until he stood close to her.

'Please come back and get the ball with me. It's really creepy in there by myself.'

Anne-Marie looked at the Forest. 'I don't want to ride home in the dark.'

'I'll come with you,' Edward said, 'if you come with me.'

It would be better than riding through the Forest by herself and anyway, getting the ball would only take a minute. Anne-Marie put her bike back onto the ground and walked up the rise to the darkened doorway.

'You really are a scaredy-cat, aren't you?' she said.

'So are you.'

Anne-Marie thought about the trees and the path underneath them.

And Maude.

'Only sometimes,' she said.

Chapter Five

Edward waited at the top of the stairs while Anne-Marie clambered down.

The air was colder and smelt like old socks down there and she had to rest her hand on the wall so she didn't stumble on the rough steps.

'Don't be too long!' Edward called. 'The ball's just there, on the landing.'

Ahead of her she could see the football where it had stopped in the corner. The stairs went down again, deeper into the ground and when Anne-Marie stooped to pick the ball up she found herself leaning further, peering into the gloom. She could see another doorway and, when she bent lower, she could see the outline of a huge fireplace.

'There's another room down here!' she called back. 'It's got a big fireplace.'

'Probably the kitchens,' Edward's voice rang out to her, bouncing off the walls. 'Hurry up. It's cold up here.'

It was cold down below, too, but Anne-Marie crept a little further on. She could never have done this in the old house at home in Australia and even in this house, this great dinosaur of a house, she could feel the prickle of gooseflesh creeping down her arms. She could almost see the cooks in the kitchen and the great centre table groaning under the weight of deer and pheasants and bundles of vegetables. She almost expected to see it and found herself listening, one ear peaked higher than the other, for the roar of the fire in the chimney. How warm it would have been then! How welcoming for a small dog in his basket. This would have been where the little dog lived. There, by the fire, in a round basket.

'Hurry up!' Edward's voice floated down again. 'What are you *doing* down there?'

Anne-Marie turned to go. 'Why don't you come down and find out?' she yelled. She heard the shuffle of Edward moving to the first step and felt a little

grin lift the corners of her mouth. She hadn't played a trick on anyone in a long time. She opened her mouth. 'OOOOOOOOooooooOOOOO!' she wailed up the stairs.

Edward yelped and Anne-Marie laughed. 'That wasn't funny!' he called down. 'I could have really hurt myself then!'

'No, you wouldn't!' She held the football tightly to her. It really was getting dark down there now and the kitchen and the darker shadows beyond were not looking quite so friendly. 'It was just a joke,' she called. 'I didn't think it would frighten you so much.'

Edward didn't answer and she rather wished she had kept her mouth shut. It was very still down there.

Her foot slipped then, just a little, as she turned, and a tiny pebble, probably a piece from the stone walls, lodged in her shoe. She bent down to free it – and saw something – something *so* soft that, for a second, she thought she had made a mistake.

She straightened up and gently, with her hand placed on the wall to stop her from tripping, again took a step down.

And there it was . . .

A soft, white blur that peeped at her from around the edge of the doorway.

Its head was cocked onto one side and one ear stood higher than the other. And its hair was long and wavy.

'Puck?'

His tiny mouth stretched into a marvellous

doggy grin and she saw him get ready to pounce on whatever it was she might throw for him.

'Come on!' Edward's voice called down again, and the little dog drew back.

Anne-Marie didn't answer. She wanted the dog to come to her, so she crouched, very still, on the fourth step from the bottom.

'Come back, Puck!' she called quietly.

But nothing happened.

She sat until she heard Edward call and then slowly climbed back up the stairs.

She kept her hand on the wall so she could look behind as she walked – and she thought she saw it once more, a soft white blur, but when she stopped and turned to go back there was nothing there.

'You took *ages*!' Edward scolded as she handed him the ball.

'There's a little dog down there,' Anne-Marie said. She still couldn't believe what she had seen. 'A little ghost dog.'

Edward looked hard at her. 'Oh, yeah! And a great big ghostie with his head chopped off, I just bet!'

Anne-Marie didn't say anything. She climbed back out through the doorway and waited until Edward had safely stuffed the football back into his anorak. Then she walked down the path and picked up her bike.

'You didn't really see a ghost dog, did you?' Edward turned around and looked at the manor house. 'In there?'

Anne-Marie nodded. 'It was there in the kitchen. In the doorway.' She was sure of it.

He looked at her as if he wanted to believe it and was busy checking out how true it could be. Then his face stopped being all creased and frowned. 'I'm not being tricked again,' he said. 'You're just making it up.' Edward climbed onto his bike, then looked back at Hollingsworth House and then again at Anne-Marie.

'You're really weird,' he said.

Chapter Six

Anne-Marie couldn't sleep.

She tossed and turned and snuggled down and tried hard to keep her eyes shut tight but nothing worked. Her eyes kept popping open and, instead of feeling tired and snoozy, she felt wide-awake.

She couldn't stop thinking about the little white dog. A *ghost* dog.

She said it over and over to herself but it made no difference. She still couldn't believe what she had seen.

Edward might have believed her if she hadn't played that dumb trick on him.

Anne-Marie didn't believe in ghosts, either. But she had seen him. With her own two eyes. And every time she thought of him she got that little twitchy excited feeling.

She twisted around in her bed. The sheets had tangled in her feet and she had to sit up to unwrap them.

Tomorrow she'd go back up to the manor house and kick a ball around with Edward. He'd better be ready if he thought she was just a dumb old girl who believed in ghosts and couldn't kick a ball!

And then, when she'd done that, she'd creep down and see if the little dog was still there.

Puck.

She floomped the sheets around. Here she was thinking about the little dog all over again. She thought about Lady Jane too, and the way they would have run and rolled together on

44

the grassy hill. It would have been hard in a long, old-fashioned dress like she must have worn but, Anne-Marie smiled, she just bet that little dog loved hanging on around the bottom of her skirts. Maude loved chasing Anne-Marie's long dressing-gown. It was no wonder Puck was still waiting there in the big kitchens.

Anne-Marie's eyes started to feel deeper, as though whatever magic makes them want to stay shut might be beginning to happen. It was no wonder . . . the pillow felt softer too . . . and her feet snugged up tighter under her tummy . . . it was no wonder Lady Jane missed him so much . . .

Anne-Marie's eyes popped open and she sat up, straight up in bed. What if . . . what if Lady Jane didn't *know* Puck was still there waiting for her? Well, how would she? She was stuck there in the village church and Puck was over on the other side of Ellersham Forest.

Oh sure! She heard her own voice talking to her inside her head. Oh, sure, it wasn't all that far from the church to the Forest – she could ride her bike along the path that led off to the left – if she was brave enough.

But back then in Lady Jane's time, her voice whispered to her, back *then* there might not have been any paths. Back then it might have seemed a long, long way to go from the church to the manor house.

Anyway, anyway, even if Lady Jane *did* know, even if Anne-Marie *did* tell her, she might not know the way any more. It would all be different now. There were cars and roads and power lines and planes and many more houses than ever there were when Lady Jane and Puck lived on the other side of the Forest.

It was just about as impossible for Lady Jane to set off and get Puck as it was for Anne-Marie to set off, over the ocean and far away, to get Maude.

'Are you still awake?' Dad stuck his head around the door. 'Is there something wrong?'

'No.' Anne-Marie hugged down into the bed. If she told Dad about the little ghost dog he'd just worry and think she was fretting about Maude.

Dad gave her a quick kiss and she listened to his footsteps thud quietly down the stairs.

She snuggled into her pillow and felt the blankets hug around her again, filling her with their gentle warmth.

Her mind drifted back to the little white dog in the kitchen of the old manor house. She wondered if he still had a basket to sleep in while he was waiting.

Like Maudie had.

Anne-Marie smiled a little: a tiny smile just for herself because something about Puck in his basket, waiting, made her feel a lot better about Maudie.

She even thought she might have felt the tiniest nudge of an idea, but the fuzz that filled her head with sleep got in the way.

Chapter Seven

When Anne-Marie had first gone to the village church she had gone in the car – being whooshed along in the back seat along an impossibly narrow road that had mist lingering in dreamy whiteness about the trees, too lazy to lift itself off the ground. But this time they were walking – her whole class, all of them rugged up in their parkas in spite of the clear, winter sun that was trying to push itself a little higher into the sky. They were going to the church to draw and to learn more about the history of the building.

She dawdled along behind the others,

cramped up in single file on the footpath with the road so close to one foot that the other foot kept getting in its way. There was more time, though, for her to peek between the empty, tangled branches of the hedgerow to see into the fields that lay beyond. So many small fields in so many greens and rich dark browns, making a giant patchwork quilt that lay across the soft hills and was stitched, here and there, with roads and fences and tufty thick lines of low bushes. It was hard to imagine, even while she looked at it, that over there was the motorway, rushing and roaring with traffic, and over that way was Hendley with its big, heated shopping-centre and its hundreds and hundreds of flats and houses. And thousands of people.

At home, in Australia, the sugarcane tumbled in pale green blankets tucked about along its sides by eucalypts and bushland. She could never walk through it like this. She would never see over the top of the tall stalks – they were even taller than the cars that drove beside them on roads that became tunnels as the cane grew higher.

Today was an adventure though and thoughts of sugarcane and hot, humid roads alongside them disappeared as a hedgehog, busy and prickled at being disturbed by so many feet, hurried importantly to a quieter sleeping-place.

Anne-Marie was looking forward to visiting the village church again as well. And she knew exactly what it was that she was going to draw. Lady Jane Latimer.

She could hardly wait and felt again the strange pulling feeling as they got closer. Almost as if Lady Jane was waiting for her.

She hadn't been back to the manor house since she fetched the football for Edward from the bottom of the stairs two weeks ago. It had rained ever since and the days had become gloomier, drizzly and damper so that a quick pedal along the path outside their house was all that could be managed before it was suddenly night, with dinner still a long way off and bed even further. There were hours to fill with a television that she didn't want to watch or books that she didn't want to read.

Just a lot of time to be bored. And to think.

It had bothered her, that rain, and she wondered if the little dog was warm down there in the dark kitchen. She wondered if he was able to stay dry.

She'd worried too that maybe Edward would tease her about the dog. She didn't want all the others at school to know about it. They wouldn't believe it anyway and they'd have something else to pick on as well as her funny way of talking.

She looked around. The others were just standing or kicking at the stones like she was.

She'd been so busy thinking about Edward and Puck and that cold, old manor house that she hadn't really noticed they'd arrived at the church.

She kicked another stone.

'Do you like our church?' a girl called Holly asked. 'Do you have churches like this in Australia?'

'I don't think so.' Anne-Marie stopped kicking her stone. The girls seemed so sure of themselves. She stood still.

The door of the church had been opened and already they were starting to herd in. Voices were quietened, except for Edward who called out that it was his turn to sit on the end, and footsteps became shuffles as they sat in the cold pews at the front of the church.

She could smell the cold. It tingled into her nose bringing with it the smell of old bricks and dusty kneeling cushions and the fragile pages of hymn books with covers that smelt like the hands of all the people who'd held them.

Mingled in with it, sweet and earthy, was the perfume that she'd smelt the other day. It called to her, and Anne-Marie looked into the darkened corner of the chapel where Lady Jane Latimer was waiting.

The crack was worse.

Anne-Marie saw it as soon as she climbed onto the step to look at the effigy of Lady Jane. There it was, running all the way across the leg of the small dog at her feet, all the way to his chest, and now it had started to move around the wavy hair in his neck.

Anne-Marie couldn't help herself. She reached over and let her fingers trace the cruel line that it made.

And she felt again the sadness that seemed to swim up at her from the figure of Lady Jane.

'He's all right.' The words whispered out of her mouth before she could stop them. It was just as well no one was near by or they would have heard her. 'I saw him.'

This time the perfume drenched the air around her. It was so strong and so sweet and Anne-Marie knew she had smelt it before, but still she couldn't remember its name. She breathed it in and tried not to look at the ugly crack in the statue of the little dog. What would happen if it opened up and the statue fell and crumbled into a pile of stones? Would Puck be all right? Or would it mean he was stuck for ever in the house on the other side of the Forest because the place where he belonged, tucked up against Lady Jane's feet, would be gone?

Her hand touched the crack and then she covered it as if she could hold it together, just for a little while – just until she knew what to do.

The perfume, sweet and peaceful, lingered around her as she reached across to the tiny circlet that lay between Lady Jane's cold, stone hands.

It's a tiny collar.

The thought popped into her head so suddenly that she heard her own breath make a sharp little '*oh*' and had to look around to check nobody else had heard. Her fingers traced the clasp and the smooth stone band that went around the dog's neck. Lady Jane must have really, really loved Puck.

She has her dog with her, Father Tom had said and it had made Anne-Marie feel better.

But now she knew he'd been wrong.

She knew Lady Jane's small dog, Puck, was waiting for her over in the manor house on the other side of the Forest.

And Lady Jane was waiting here.

No wonder she looked so sad.

The perfume tingled at her nose and Anne-Marie looked around to make sure nobody was standing close. She didn't want anybody to see her talking to a statue.

But she had to say it.

She had to find out.

'Do you want me to bring Puck to you?' she whispered. She felt her face go bright pink and tried not to think how silly it was to talk to a stone statue in a church.

She climbed down quickly. Even sillier, she decided, to say she was going to bring Puck here when she had no idea, no idea at all, about how she was going to do that.

She started to walk away, to go somewhere else to draw a vase or a pew or another statue or something, but the perfume, so strong that she was sure everyone would turn around and look to see where it was coming from, stopped her.

And the circlet, the tiny dog's collar, dropped to the step and rolled down to the floor and didn't stop rolling until it lay, in its perfect little stone circle, at her feet.

Chapter Eight

Anne-Marie held onto the tiny stone circlet all through the next day. When it wasn't in her hands it was in the pocket of her skirt, snugly wrapped in her handkerchief. She wasn't sure yet what she was going to do with it – it certainly wasn't going to fit around a ghost dog's neck. Even if it could it would be like putting a collar on a cloud. And how would you lead a cloud along, anyway?

It was just too hard to think about for long. Her stomach got itself tied up in knots. She tried, though, and sat all through lunch break on one of the seats at the side of the playground. It was freezing but her hands were warm, snugged into her pocket so she could hold, more tightly, the stone circlet.

'Do you want to come and play?' Holly held the netball under her arm. 'You can play up the other end.'

Anne-Marie looked up. She'd never be able to play as well as they did. And she didn't really know the rules. She'd probably run the wrong way, or go over the line or something stupid.

She held the circlet tightly. She couldn't play. She might lose it.

Anne-Marie shook her head.

'She won't play!' Holly bellowed across the playground. 'She's sitting sulking about dumb old Australia!'

'I am not!' Anne-Marie wanted to jump up and push her, really hard. She wasn't sulking about Australia. It was better than dumb old England anyway.

'What *are* you doing then?' A girl called Tracey joined in. 'You can't just sit there.'

She was guarding a circlet. 'I can if I want to.' She huddled down a bit further until the collar of her anorak was sitting under her nose. Just wait until she took Puck home to Lady Jane! Just wait until then, she wanted to yell!

Then she'd play! Only she wouldn't play dumb old netball.

No-siree! She'd play football with Edward and she'd barge right through the middle of their stupid netball court.

That'd show them!

Anne-Marie had gone to bed early. Perhaps it would be easier to solve the problem of fetching a little ghost dog with a collar only as big as a pinkie ring if she was lying down. It looked up at her now from its hiding place beside her pillow. Tomorrow she'd take it and go back to the manor house.

Maybe she could get Puck to follow her if she showed it to him.

Maybe that was why it had dropped from Lady Jane's stone hands, but Anne-Marie really didn't think so. It was just Lady Jane telling her how much she missed her small dog and how much she wanted him back.

There *had* to be a way though – some way that she could make Puck follow her along the path to the church. There was no way she could pick him up or drag him along behind her.

'I found something for you at the markets today.' Her dad popped his head around the door. 'I thought it might help you sleep.'

He held out a tiny lace bag with a ribbon around the top. When Anne-Marie reached out and took it she heard the soft scrunch of dried petals inside the bag and she smelt their perfume.

It wafted out to her, calling her as it had down at the church.

'Oh!' said Anne-Marie. 'It's just exactly what I wanted.'

Of course! It was lavender! Hadn't she smelt it in Nan's bedroom all scrunched up in the drawer where she kept her knickers and singlets? It was even in her own garden at home.

Her dad was looking very pleased with himself. 'If you put it under your pillow it's supposed to give you sweet dreams. I don't know about that but it certainly smells nice.'

'It smells wonderful!' Anne-Marie jumped up and gave him a hug.

'Put it under your pillow then!' her dad laughed.

She bounced herself back under the covers. 'Soon I will,' she grinned up at him. 'I want to hold it for a while – and smell it.'

She would put it under there later but she didn't think it would help her sleep. It would remind her of tomorrow and how she was going to take it, and the circlet, into the dark kitchen of the manor house to find the little dog Puck.

She just bet that Puck would know this smell, this lovely lavender smell.

Just like Maudie knew the special Anne-Marie smell of the old jumper in the bottom of her basket.

Anne-Marie hugged herself tight and did a little bouncy twist around in her bed.

She could hardly wait for tomorrow.

Chapter Nine

Edward was there when Anne-Marie rode her bike onto the path below Hollingsworth House.

'What are *you* doing here again?' he called.

Anne-Marie watched while he found a stick to prod his football out of a mud puddle.

The manor house loomed high above them, its giant walls reaching to the sky and the shadows inside already deepening in the late afternoon light. Over to one side the path led off again, in a different direction. Somewhere down there, along that path, was the village church.

'I've come to show you how to kick a ball!'

'Oh, right!' Edward dumped the ball in front of him and rolled it around a bit to get some of the mud off. 'I suppose you're really good at it.'

'Better than you, anyway.' Anne-Marie jumped off her bike. She ran hard and the muddy ground squelched and splashed patterns onto her track pants. But it felt good.

She slammed her foot out and sent the ball sailing across the ground, running so hard that her breath made puffing round shapes ahead of her in the cold air.

In her pocket, beneath her hand, she held tightly to the lavender bag and the tiny stone circlet.

Edward puffed up the rise to where she stood with the ball at her feet.

'I'll show you how to kick it if you take me over to the church when we've finished,' she said. She did a quick little turn and nipped the ball out to the side.

Edward let it go. He looked down the path and then back to Anne-Marie. 'What do you want to go there for?'

Anne-Marie shrugged. He wouldn't believe her even if she told him that she was going to lead a little ghost dog along the path to the chapel at the back of the church. 'I just want to go and have a look, that's all.'

'It won't be any good,' Edward said. 'It'll be locked up.'

For a second Anne-Marie felt her heart sink right down into the bottom of her stomach. She hadn't thought of it being locked up.

'Won't Father Tom be there?'

Edward prodded at the ball. 'I don't know.' He looked hard at Anne-Marie. 'What do you *really* want to go there for?'

Anne-Marie took a deep breath and her hands closed even more tightly around the little stone circlet. 'I have to put something back,' she said.

'Like what?' Edward moved a bit closer.

'This.' Anne-Marie held out the circlet for Edward to see.

Edward's eyes went very round. So did his mouth. He made a few huffing sounds. 'You'll really cop it!' he said. 'You're not allowed to take things out of churches!'

'I didn't take it!' Anne-Marie felt herself going pink. She didn't think that she had been stealing. She had only taken it so she could lead Puck home to Lady Jane. 'It fell into my shoe.'

Edward looked at her shoes and then at her face.

'I want to put it back,' she said.

'*I'm* not helping.' Edward picked up the ball. 'I already copped it when the hymn book fell to bits. And I didn't even *do* anything.'

He started to walk down the hill. And then he stopped. He looked up at Anne-Marie and then at the muddy ball in his arms. 'Can you really show me how to kick like that?' he said.

Anne-Marie nodded. 'I can show you how to make the ball go where you want it to. You can already kick it okay.'

'All right.' Edward walked back. 'But I'm only going to the gate. You can go and get Father Tom by yourself.'

Anne-Marie grinned. She tucked the stone circlet into her pocket with the lavender bag and zipped it up.

All she had to do now was send the ball into the manor house and, when she went to get it, somehow bring Puck out with her.

Chapter Ten

'Not again!' Edward howled when the ball sailed through the doors of the manor house. 'I'm not going in there to get it!'

Anne-Marie had already run past him. She had her anorak tied around her middle and her face felt hot but it had been good playing football again. Running and bumping and charging.

And now she was going in to find Puck.

'I'll get it!' she called as she climbed through the doorway. 'You start walking with the bikes. I'll catch up.' She thought about the shadowy path beneath the Forest trees. 'And go slow!'

She waited until she saw Edward juggling the

bikes along the path and then moved further into the gloomy darkness of the big hall.

Ahead of her were the stairs that led down to the kitchen.

Quickly she picked up the football and then took the lavender bag and stone circlet from her pocket and crept down to the first landing.

It was so cold down there. The air touched her hot cheeks like trickles of icy water.

'Puck!' she called quietly and held out the lavender bag. 'Come on, Puck. Come and see what I've got.'

For a little while nothing happened. Only the shadows seemed to move and make darker corners around the doorway below her.

Anne-Marie squeezed the lavender bag, shook it a little and then sniffed at the air to see if its perfume was reaching out for the ghost dog as it had reached out to her in the church.

She called gently again.

A tiny white mist appeared in one of the deep shadows near the doorway and she thought she heard a growling sound.

'It's me,' she said. 'Come and see what I've got.'

The white mist moved out a little and she saw the long wavy coat that fell to the floor. Now she could see two ears, one as before cocked higher than the other, and two bright eyes.

'Come on,' she said.

The misty little dog moved forward. His nose was pointed high as if he were scenting something and suddenly, so suddenly that Anne-Marie nearly toppled off her step, he bounded forward. She heard a joyful yapping sound, a small sound, and he ran around and around and around, chasing his raggy tail.

Anne-Marie held out the circlet for him to sniff. She stayed perfectly still while the small bundle of mist inched closer.

'Are you coming or not?' Edward's voice drifted down to her. 'It's cold out here and it's

too hard to push two bikes by myself!' He must have come back.

The tiny dog had heard it too and fled away down the stairs. It disappeared into the darkest shadow on the other side of the door.

Anne-Marie glanced up the steps. She should call out to Edward – she should say, 'Hold on. I won't be a minute!' She should say anything, but Puck mightn't come out again if her voice was too loud. It was so, so quiet down there.

'Oh, *please*,' Anne-Marie whispered into the darkness. 'Oh please, you have to come *now*.'

Soon it would be too dark, much too dark even to kid Edward that she needed to go to the church. She held out the lavender bag again, and again she snuffled the flowers inside to send the perfume drifting out.

'Come on, Puck.' She made coaxing noises and shook the bag hard.

Around her the shadows now were so dark it was difficult to see the bottom of the stairs.

But she stayed, calling and coaxing until the little white dog peeked out. If he didn't come soon she'd have to leave.

'You have to come with me now,' she said. 'Come on, Puck!'

The little dog inched forward, following the

scent that Anne-Marie squeezed out of her lavender bag.

It was then she noticed that the small dog was
limping badly. She longed to reach out and pick
him up, but even if he would let her, she wasn't
sure it was possible to pick up a dog who was
really only a bundle of mist.

'Are you hurt?' she said as she coaxed him up
another stair.

The little dog followed slowly, sniffing at the
perfume and the circlet that were held out to
him.

Anne-Marie thought of the crack in the
statue at the church.

She didn't like to think what
might happen when the crack
got higher and wider and bigger and the whole statue crumbled into dust.

It would be too awful if the
tiny dog disappeared before she
could take him to Lady Jane.

Anne-Marie knew that they
couldn't wait until tomorrow. She *had*
to get him out now, so she whispered and called
and all the time kept climbing, one tiny step at a
time.

Chapter Eleven

Anne-Marie didn't dare look around when she reached the doorway of the old house. It loomed high ahead of her and the icy wind tore up the rise and chilled through her track top and into her shoulders. She tugged her anorak from around her waist and untangled it, ready to pull it on.

The little dog stopped.

'Come on, Puck.' Anne-Marie crept over the fallen stones at her feet, feeling her way. 'It's not far.'

His leg was hurting. She could see now how he was lifting his paw and holding it out almost as if he wanted her to fix it for him. She thought of the crack in the stone statue in the church and the cruel way it ran from the top of one shoulder right across the front leg – the same leg that Puck was holding up now.

'Come on, Puck boy.' She reached her hand out, palm up, beckoning him. She didn't dare go too close. What if he ran back now?

'It's not far,' she whispered. 'Try just a little bit harder. Come on, come on, Puck.'

Gently she stooped down and tied the circlet and the lavender bag into the cord of her anorak. She longed to put it on but this way she could trail the circlet and the bag behind her. It would give the little dog something to follow.

Around her the day had disappeared behind the heavy grey sky. Daytime shadows now were mixing in with the shadows of night. Soon it would be really dark.

Anne-Marie turned and let her anorak drag onto the ground. Her mother would be cross because already it was muddy, but it was going to work – the little dog put his head on one side, then began to follow. He sat again and then he scampered a few steps, like it was a game that he knew, following her down the path that led to the Forest and the church.

And he kept coming. Following her.

'Good dog,' she was saying over and over again. Just like she did with Maude. 'Good dog, Puck boy. Good, good dog.'

It was colder in the Forest. And darker. And the trees whispered their sad, bare branches together as she passed by. She saw her bike on the path, left there by Edward when he'd obviously got sick of waiting for her, and she walked around it.

She wished he *had* waited. She could have made him believe it if he'd waited and he could have helped. But he probably thought she was just playing another trick on him. He must have been really angry.

She dangled the cord of her anorak a little harder.

Well, what did she expect? She wasn't really his friend. Not like her friends in Australia. They wouldn't have gone off and left her in a dark place just because she played one little trick.

'Come on, good dog,' she coaxed him and then let the cord stay still for a minute while he sat down to rest his paw. She set off again along the path just as soon as he was on his feet.

He wasn't scampering now – just limping slowly. He stopped every now and then to look back, as if he knew that already he had come too far from the only place he knew.

'You'll be all right.' Anne-Marie tried not to think about how much his leg must be hurting. 'Come on. It's not much further.'

Puck looked up at her and she heard the softest whimper pass by, like the brush of a breeze against her cheek. A sad sound. She shook the lavender bag on the end of the cord again. She *had* to make him walk and it hurt her to think about it. 'You *have* to keep going.'

He was looking up at her, like Maudie did, with his tiny, misty head always on one side. Almost as if he knew she was sad too.

'Come on,' she urged. And tried to make herself smile. Maudie liked it best when she smiled. It made her run over and leap and play again. 'Let's have another game.'

'That's better,' she said. 'Try and catch the cord. Come on, Puck.' It was really hurting him but Anne-Marie kept coaxing. The cold ached into her bones and she longed to bounce and jump, to make her blood flow pink and warm into her fingers. It was so cold her feet hurt and great hiccupping shivers raced up her back.

She looked away from Puck for a second, back over her shoulder. She really had no idea where they were, only that it had taken ever so long to get there. She could see now that the path widened in front of her and the trees held their branches back a little so she could make out the clearing ahead.

The churchyard. And the wall. And the gravestones.

Beyond them lay the church, and Anne-Marie could tell, even from here, that it was all locked up. Tight and still and ready for the night.

Her heart sank a little as she stood looking up at it.

If only Edward had stayed . . .

Chapter Twelve

The wind was waiting for Anne-Marie out in the churchyard and it pulled and pressed at her track top and sneaked its mean, cold fingers around her throat.

She shivered hard now. Her teeth made little chattering noises.

She was sure she'd have to take her anorak back so she could hug the parts that weren't too muddy around her. She tugged at it gently and was pleased when the small dog moved closer. He seemed to be sniffing, his nose lifted high into the wind.

Anne-Marie smelt it then, too. The sweet,

stronger smell of lavender. Only this time it was mixed with other smells that were perhaps petticoats and dresses and the soap smell that was always left when hair was washed and clean.

The misty little dog ran towards the church, lifting his paw every now and then and turning to make funny barking, yapping noises as if to tell Anne-Marie to hurry, to come with him to the door.

Anne-Marie ran behind, hugging her anorak on as she went and ignoring the big muddy splotch that was the hood.

The dog was pawing at the door now and Anne-Marie pressed behind him, leaning hard against the old, oak timbers to try and make it open. The wind whipped around them and she felt the lump come back to her throat. Sad whining sounds reached up from the misty little dog at her feet and she felt big, hot tears trickle onto her cheeks.

To get this far, so close . . .

She banged her hands hard now onto the church door and the air around them filled with perfume. Even the wind seemed to help, pressing its breath against the heavy timber and the church wall.

More than anything Anne-Marie wanted that

great, heavy door to open.

Her hands hurt, a stinging hurt from beating so hard, and her fingers throbbed from the cold so that she had to stop for a minute. The dog was quiet too. And still. There was only the sound of the wind and even that seemed to settle for a second to let a new sound reach her.

Voices.

Coming closer.

Puck huddled into the darkest shadow and Anne-Marie stepped in front of him. She scrubbed the tears from her face and turned around.

'I told you she'd be here!' Edward. Good old, wonderful old Edward. He stood pointing at her from the bottom of the churchyard. 'See! I told you!' He ran over to Anne-Marie. 'What were you *doing*? I called and called and you didn't answer and I thought you'd probably fallen down the steps or something.' He was looking at her knees as if he expected to see scrapes and bruises. 'Did you hurt yourself much?'

Other people were running to her now.

'I couldn't get out,' she said. It was nearly the truth and, if he hadn't seen the white mist that hovered behind her legs, well . . . it would be just too hard to explain right now. 'I thought you were mad at me.'

Edward's mum got there first. 'I rang your mother straight away, Anne-Marie. Edward was in such a state. I thought the house must have fallen in on top of you.' She gave Edward a hug.

Edward squeezed himself free. 'Get off it, Mum.' He shook his anorak back into place.

'I'm freezing.' Anne-Marie shivered great shuddery shivers. 'I had to come here,' she said. 'See, there's this statue in there . . .' Where to begin . . . where to start to try and explain.

Anne-Marie's dad arrived next and then poor Father Tom who looked like an enormous caped wonder as the wind tore at his cassock.

'We were so worried!'

'Where have you been?'

'What are you doing here?'

They all asked at once and she felt herself being wrapped in scarves and hoods and woollen beanies and her father's hands rubbing and rubbing and deliciously warming her. Nobody slowed down enough to let her answer any of their questions.

And under it all, at the back of her legs, she could feel the cold misty shape of Puck huddling harder against the wall.

'Let's get out of the wind.' Father Tom pulled

an enormous key from his pocket and turned it in the lock on the door.

The dark, empty stillness of the church was refrigerator-cold as Anne-Marie stepped through, following the scampering, bounding bundle of mist that ran ahead of her.

Puck raced up the centre aisle, his sore leg forgotten as he leapt onto a pew and along it. Father Tom had clicked on the lights and they made such a mixture of light and dark and jewelled brightness that a small lighter-than-light foggy mist was easily overlooked.

Anne-Marie watched as Puck crossed into the darkened corner of the chapel and made one final leap to sit at Lady Jane's feet. He turned and looked back to Anne-Marie, his paw lifted, and she saw, she *knew* she saw, the biggest doggy smile she'd ever seen in her whole life.

The air filled, in a sudden rush, with the perfumes of all the field flowers, of roses and lavender and nodding violets and the forest smell of wild thyme.

And then Puck was gone.

Only Edward spoke. 'Did someone put some flowers in here or something?' he said.

Edward hadn't left her back there in the manor house. He hadn't just run off – he'd gone to get help.

Anne-Marie laughed. A wonderful laugh that bubbled right down from deep in her tummy. She gave Edward the biggest crunchy-punch on his arm. The first one since she'd come to England.

'No! It's not flowers!' She wanted to tell him that it was the scent of a feeling. It was the explosion of happiness that Lady Jane felt when Puck came back. The same feeling she would feel when she went home to Maude.

It was a reward for being away from some-thing you loved for a very long time. Something that would make all the hard bits worthwhile.

But it was too difficult to tell about that now.

'Of course it's not flowers,' she giggled. 'There aren't any vases, you daft thing!'

Edward grinned. 'Hey! Did you hear that?' He looked at his mother. 'She sounds just like we do! Go on . . .' he said, pointing at Anne-Marie. 'Say "daft thing" again!'

He was teasing her but this time she didn't mind.

She was too full of the scent of flowers – and another feeling. A new feeling that was mixed up with a little ghost dog and a chapel in a church in a strange country.

And a boy who cared about her, even if she was different.

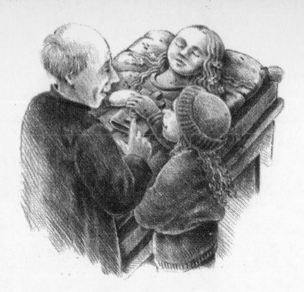

Chapter Thirteen

Before they left the church Anne-Marie walked over to the chapel and placed the tiny stone circlet back under the hands of Lady Jane Latimer.

'You shouldn't have worried so much,' Father Tom said when she showed it to him. 'Edward told us that you were going to come back here tonight. You could have given it to me at school tomorrow.'

They were standing together on the step looking at the statue of Lady Jane.

'It's really strange,' Father Tom went on. 'I never imagined that it would come loose.' He stood back a little. 'It's all so old though. I suppose some parts of it are starting to wear. Look . . .' He moved closer to the statue of Puck. 'There's a crack starting . . .'

He stopped. Anne-Marie moved closer to see what it was that made him look so carefully at the statue.

'There *was* a crack in this,' he said. 'Right there.' His fingers walked from the dog's paw to its shoulder and then across its back. 'It's not there now.'

He bent down to look more closely.

Anne-Marie didn't. Lady Jane and Puck were together again and so were their statues.

'How strange.' Father Tom looked back to the circlet under Lady Jane's fingers. 'Perhaps the stones moved,' he said. 'I shall have to take care and make sure that this doesn't roll away again. It would be awful if we lost it.'

His fingers touched it, as if he were testing to see if it was safe.

The circlet didn't budge.

'Well, I never! Now how on earth did that come loose before?'

He looked hard at Anne-Marie. And then at Lady Jane.

'Do you know . . .' he said. 'I think she looks

a whole lot happier tonight, don't you?'

'I think she does too,' Anne-Marie said as she jumped down. 'Maybe she knows . . .' she called out as she clattered into the aisle towards her dad, '. . . that Puck had never stopped waiting for her.'

'Puck?' Father Tom called out. 'Who's Puck?'

Anne-Marie looked at her dad. 'It's a name . . .' Anne-Marie's dad said, '. . . that was written on our bathroom mirror one night.'

'Really? My word.' Father Tom held the door open for them to go out into the cold, dark English evening. 'What a strange place to write!'

Anne-Marie did a little bounce from one foot to the other, trying to keep the cold out. 'It sure is!' she said.

As she raced down the path to the car she thought she smelt one last, tiny giggle of lavender.

She smiled back.

'I'm starved!' she said as she clambered into the car with her dad. 'Let's go home!'

Chapter Fourteen

Anne-Marie taped down the last piece of paper on Maudie's parcel. Tomorrow Dad was going to post it and one day next week it would arrive at Nan's house back in Australia. She tried to imagine Pop opening it and smiled when she thought about how he would tell Maude who it was from.

'It's from Anne-Marie,' he would say and let her sniff it. And Maudie would remember. She probably didn't even need Pop to remind her.

Puck hadn't had anyone to remind him about Lady Jane and he'd never forgotten her.

She'd finished her letter to Colleen as well, her

best friend back home, and told her about going to the church for art lessons. And about Edward and kicking the ball and the old manor house.

Anne-Marie thought about Holly at her English school. Tomorrow it might be easier to say *yes* if they asked her to join in. And if she didn't ask ... well ... maybe if she hung around the edge of the game somebody would.

Or she could ask them.

She could start kicking a soccer ball around all by herself. She just bet it wouldn't take too long before they'd all join in. And there was always Edward after school and the football at the manor house. They could ride their bikes along the Forest paths too. There were lots of paths and it was more fun if somebody else was there.

Edward said he wasn't going to play if she went charging into the manor house again. He didn't like standing around on the outside by himself.

Anne-Marie smiled.

She wouldn't be going into the manor house again. It was just a big, old, empty shell of a building with a hill in front of it that was good for kicking a football.

That hill'd probably be good for rolling down when the ground dried out a bit. In summer.

Anne-Marie looked at the calendar.

Summer was a long way off. But not as far as December and the plane trip that would take her home.

Anne-Marie put the parcel and the letter on the bench so Dad wouldn't forget to mail them.

The calendar on the wall looked back at her, fat with all the months that lay ahead. She'd forgotten to mark off the days. She'd been so busy thinking about Puck and Lady Jane that the days had passed all by themselves.

'What are you doing?' Anne-Marie's mum asked. She saw the parcel on the bench. 'You're not worrying about Maudie, are you?'

Anne-Marie touched the parcel. 'No,' she said. 'I was thinking about summer and riding the bikes through the Forest and football and netball and rolling down that hill near the manor house. It'd be a good hill to roll down. And Father Tom said they have tug-of-war over the headstones . . .'

'Wow,' Dad said. 'You sound like you're going to be pretty busy.'

Anne-Marie put her pencil down. 'Yep,' she said. 'From now on I think I will be.'

She gave Maudie's parcel one last pat.

Even if she hadn't hidden old dirty socks

inside it, Anne-Marie knew now, for sure and certain, Maudie would never forget her.

They'd just miss each other for a little while, that's all.

About the author

Nette Hilton was born in Traralgon, Victoria and has since lived in many different places in Australia and England. She continues to combine her two careers of teaching and writing. Among her ever popular and highly successful books are *A Proper Little Lady* (shortlisted for the Children's Book Council of Australia's Book of the Year award), *The Web* and *The Long Red Scarf* (both Honour Books in the Children's Book Council of Australia's Book of the Year awards), *The Belonging of Emmaline Harris* and *Four Eyes*.

Nette shares her life with her husband and children and many furred and feathered friends – one of whom is a raggy old poodle named Maude.

About the illustrator

A true creative traveller, Chantal Stewart was born in Paris and has devoted her life to art. She began at the Ecole Des Arts Appliques (School of Applied Arts) in Paris and worked in France as a graphic designer and illustrator.

In 1970 she studied etching at Ottawa University and then moved to Australia in 1981. For the past ten years Chantal has lived in Melbourne and her work has appeared in many different design, advertising and publishing projects, including educational books and her first children's picture book, *Percy* by R. Dunn, which was shortlisted for the Children's Book Council of Australia's Crichton Award. Another of her picture books, *Smelly Chantelly* by Joan Van Loon, was shortlisted in the YABBA awards.

Chantal currently works overlooking a lush garden in Eltham on the outskirts of Melbourne.

MORE GREAT READING FROM PUFFIN

☆☆☆☆☆☆☆☆☆☆☆☆☆☆☆☆☆☆☆☆☆☆☆☆☆☆☆☆☆☆

ALSO BY NETTE HILTON

The Belonging of Emmaline Harris   Illustrated by John Burge

Emmaline Harris's father has just moved interstate with his new wife and their new baby. And Emmaline's mum is going to marry Doug Grenfell. So where does that leave Emmaline? Where does *she* belong? Here is a moving, gently humorous story from this popular Australian author.

Britt the Boss   Margaret Clark/
              Illustrated by Bettina Guthridge

You might know some bossy people, but no one compares to Bossy Boots Britt at Mango Street Primary! Here's another hilarious story about everyone's favourite group of kids.

Copycat   Margaret Clark/illustrated by Bettina Guthridge

Justin Day is the most brilliant copycat in the whole class. His eyeballs are always on the prowl, sneaking a look at anyone's work, copying everrything and everyone. He's a walking, talking photocopier! But Crystal Baulle is on the look-out and she decides to do something about Justin's annoying habit.

Not Again, Dad!   Thurley Fowler/Illustrated by Craig Smith

Paul knew how to manage Mum, but when she's away and Dad becomes household manager, it isn't so easy. The worst part is when Dad joins in on cricket and swimming classes – totally embarrassing!

MORE GREAT READING FROM PUFFIN

☆ ☆

The Bugalugs Bum Thief
Tim Winton/Illustrated by Carol Pelham-Thorman

A small fishing town is electrified when all the bums are stolen one dark night – stolen by the Bugalugs bum thief – and when they are finally located all hell breaks loose.

A Children's Book Council of Australia Notable Book, 1992.

So Who Needs Lotto?   Libby Hathorn/Illustrated by Simon Kneebone

When Denise Albermarle arrives at Mimosa Primary School, she is such a show-off and a bully that everyone hates her. So when she begins to strike up a friendship with shy Cosmo Ravezzi, no one is more surprised than he is . . .

A Children's Book Council of Australia Notable Book, 1991.

Old Tom at the Beach   Leigh Hobbs

In this second book in the Old Tom series, he and Angela spend a day at the beach. Angela just begins to relax when Old Tom gets swept out to sea . . . Old Tom is irresistible in his flippers and snorkel!

The Burnt Stick   Anthony Hill/Illustrated by Mark Sofilas

A beautifully written and illustrated novella about the strength of the human spirit. An Aboriginal boy struggles to decide where he belongs and how he can cope with a society that didn't understand and didn't tolerate.

MORE GREAT READING FROM PUFFIN

☆☆☆☆☆☆☆☆☆☆☆☆☆☆☆☆☆☆☆☆☆☆☆☆☆☆☆☆☆☆

I Hate Fridays   Rachel Flynn/Illustrated by Craig Smith

A collection of stories about characters in the classroom, about all the funny, sad and traumatic things that can happen. Hilariously illustrated by the very popular Craig Smith.

A Children's Book Council of Australia Notable Book, 1991.

It's Not Fair!   Rachel Flynn/Illustrated by Craig Smith

Following *I Hate Fridays*, here is another outstanding collection of true-to-life stories from the characters at Koala Hills.

I Can't Wait!   Rachel Flynn/Illustrated by Craig Smith

It's the last year of primary school for the characters from Koala Hills. Following the huge success of *I Hate Fridays* and *It's Not Fair!*, here are your favourite characters back again.

Worried Sick   Rachel Flynn/Illustrated by Craig Smith

The characters from Koala Hills have now entered the minefield of secondary school in this, the fourth book in the hugely successful I Hate Fridays series.

MORE GREAT READING FROM PUFFIN

☆ ☆

Unbelievable! Paul Jennings

You'll never guess what's going to happen, because these stories are unbelievable!

Winner of the 1988 Young Australians' Best Book Award (YABBA), Victoria.
Winner of the 1991 Kids Reading Oz Choice Award (KROC), NT.

Quirky Tails Paul Jennings

Eight hilarious oddball stories, each one as larrikin and bizarre as the other, and each with a twist in the tail.

Winner of the 1992 Young Australians' Best Book Award (YABBA), Victoria.

Undone! Paul Jennings

Plans come undone. Zips come undone. Bullies come undone. And so will the readers who try to predict the endings of these eight weird and wonderful stories.

Winner of the 1993 Kids Reading Oz Choice Award (KROC), NT.

Spooner or Later Paul Jennings, Ted Greenwood/ Illustrated by Terry Denton

It's largely loopy, a touch over the top, and it'll drive you crazy. But for those who like a laugh and a challenge, *Spooner or Later* will lead you on a wonderfully wacky hunt for the Reverend Spooner's watched birds (oops . . . *botched words!*).

Winner of the 1993 Joyce Nicholson Award for the Best Designed Book and the 1993 Award for the Best Designed Children's Book of the Year.